Dear Parents:

Congratulations! Your child is taking the first steps on an exciting journey. The destination? Independent reading!

STEP INTO READING® will help your child get there. The program offers five steps to reading success. Each step includes fun stories and colorful art or photographs. In addition to original fiction and books with favorite characters, there are Step into Reading Non-Fiction Readers, Phonics Readers and Boxed Sets, Sticker Readers, and Comic Readers—a complete literacy program with something to interest every child.

Learning to Read, Step by Step!

Ready to Read   Preschool–Kindergarten
• big type and easy words • rhyme and rhythm • picture clues
For children who know the alphabet and are eager to begin reading.

Reading with Help   Preschool–Grade 1
• basic vocabulary • short sentences • simple stories
For children who recognize familiar words and sound out new words with help.

Reading on Your Own   Grades 1–3
• engaging characters • easy-to-follow plots • popular topics
For children who are ready to read on their own.

Reading Paragraphs   Grades 2–3
• challenging vocabulary • short paragraphs • exciting stories
For newly independent readers who read simple sentences with confidence.

Ready for Chapters   Grades 2–4
• chapters • longer paragraphs • full-color art
For children who want to take the plunge into chapter books but still like colorful pictures.

STEP INTO READING® is designed to give every child a successful reading experience. The grade levels are only guides; children will progress through the steps at their own speed, developing confidence in their reading. The F&P Text Level on the back cover serves as another tool to help you choose the right book for your child.

Remember, a lifetime love of reading starts with a single step!

*To Grampap. To Samantha, who put me
in puppy heaven. And to Skippy, Brownie,
Terry, Shadow, Bud, Zipper, Punk, Charlie,
and all the pets who enrich our lives.*
—V.M.N.

For my pup, Oliver Bean
—D.A.

Text copyright © 2024 by Vaunda Micheaux Nelson
Cover art and interior illustrations copyright © 2024 by Derek Anderson

All rights reserved. Published in the United States by Random House Children's Books, a division
of Penguin Random House LLC, New York.

Step into Reading, Random House, and the Random House colophon are registered trademarks
of Penguin Random House LLC.

Visit us on the Web!
rhcbooks.com

Educators and librarians, for a variety of teaching tools, visit us at RHTeachersLibrarians.com

Library of Congress Cataloging-in-Publication Data
Names: Nelson, Vaunda Micheaux, author. | Anderson, Derek, illustrator.
Title: Ready? Set. Puppies! / by Vaunda Micheaux Nelson ; illustrated by Derek Anderson.
Description: First edition. | New York : Random House, [2024] | Series: Step into reading |
Audience: Ages 4–6. | Summary: Raymond and Roxy wait for Flo to give birth to her puppies.
Identifiers: LCCN 2022059926 (print) | LCCN 2022059927 (ebook) |
ISBN 978-0-593-56377-9 (trade paperback) | ISBN 978-0-593-56378-6 (library binding) |
ISBN 978-0-593-56379-3 (ebook)
Subjects: CYAC: Dogs—Fiction. | Animals—Infancy—Fiction. | LCGFT: Picture books.
Classification: LCC PZ7.N43773 Rd 2024 (print) | LCC PZ7.N43773 (ebook) | DDC [Fic]—dc21

Printed in the United States of America
10 9 8 7 6 5 4 3
First Edition

This book has been officially leveled by using the F&P Text Level Gradient™ Leveling System.

STEP INTO READING®

STEP 2

READING WITH HELP

READY? SET. PUPPIES!

◆A RAYMOND AND ROXY BOOK◆

by Vaunda Micheaux Nelson

illustrated by Derek Anderson

Random House 🏠 New York

Slow Flo

Raymond has a cat named Flash.

Roxy has a dog named Flo.

Flash and Flo
like to run fast
together.
But Flo is
slowing down.

"Flo's belly is bigger," Raymond says.

"Flo is going to have puppies," says Roxy.

"Oh boy!" says Raymond.

Raymond pats Flo.

Flo wags her tail.

Her big belly sways

back and forth.

Roxy rubs Flo's head.
She looks sideways
at Raymond and says,
"The puppies
will need homes."

Raymond jumps up.

"I want one!" he says.

Please!

Raymond bursts
into the house.
"Flo is going to
have puppies, Mama!
May we keep one?"

Mama is reading
a book.

She does not look up.

"We already have
Flash," she says.

"Flash wants a puppy,
too," Raymond says.
Mama closes her book.
"Oh really?" Mama says.

"He told me," says Raymond.

Mama laughs.

"Please?" Raymond begs.

"We will see," Mama says.

The Long Wait

On Monday,
Raymond darts
next door.

"Did Flo have
    her pups?" he asks.
"Not yet," Roxy says.
"Hurry up, puppies!"
    he tells Flo's belly.

On Tuesday,
Raymond zips
next door.
"Did her puppies come?"
"No," Roxy says.

The puppies do not come on Wednesday, Thursday, or Friday.

On Saturday,
Raymond bolts
next door.

"Raymond! Raymond!"

Roxy spins him around.

"The pups are coming!"

"Flo is hiding,"
Roxy says.
"Ma says Flo wants
to be alone
to have her puppies."
"Oh boy!" says Raymond.

Puppies!

On Sunday, Roxy calls.

"The puppies are here!"

Raymond flies outside.

Flash races with him.

Flo is in a box
in Roxy's garage.
Raymond counts
five puppies
cuddled with Flo.

"They are all sleeping,"
  Raymond says.

"They are not asleep,"
  says Roxy.

"Ma says their eyes
  do not open at first."

Raymond likes the
brown puppy
with the white stripe.
"Hello, Streak!"
Raymond says.

Roxy laughs.

"Streak?

You named him fast."

"I did," Raymond says.

Streak

Raymond visits Streak
every day.

One day his eyes open.

"Streak can see us now,"
Raymond says.

Flash meows.

He sniffs Streak.

They touch noses.

They like each other.

Raymond dashes home.

"Guess what, Mama?

Flash likes Streak!

And Streak likes Flash!"

Mama looks at Papa.

"Let's go see," she says.

Raymond and Flash run

ahead of them.

Mama and Streak
touch noses.
Streak licks her face.
"I think I'm in love,"
Mama says.

"I guess we have
 a new puppy," says Papa.
"Oh boy!" Raymond says.
"Thank you! Thank you!"

Raymond is
in love, too.